When You Hug My Pillow

Michael A. Campbell

Order this book online at www.trafford.com
or email orders@trafford.com

Most Trafford titles are also available at major online book retailers.

Print information available on the last page.

ISBN: 978-1-4907-9196-8 (sc)

978-1-4907-9197-5 (e)

Our mission is to efficiently provide the world's finest, most comprehensive book publishing service, enabling every author to experience success. To find out how to publish your book, your way, and have it available worldwide, visit us online at www.trafford.com

Any people depicted in stock imagery provided by Getty Images are models, and such images are being used for illustrative purposes only.
Certain stock imagery © Getty Images.

Trafford rev. 11/06/2018

Trafford PUBLISHING® www.trafford.com

North America & international
toll-free: 1 888 232 4444 (USA & Canada)
fax: 812 355 4082

Dedicated to: Christian Campbell aka Nook Nook

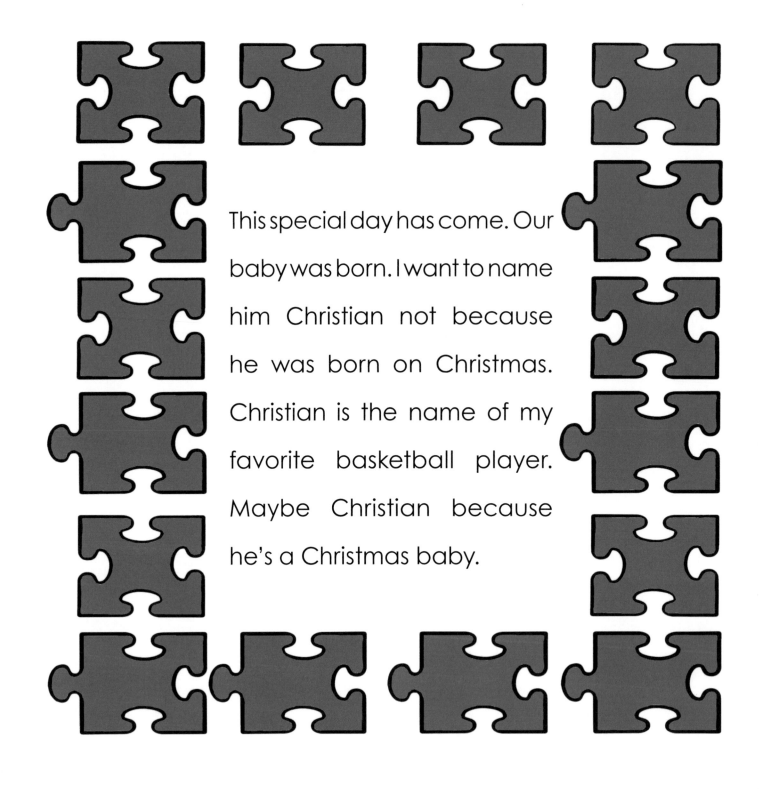

This special day has come. Our baby was born. I want to name him Christian not because he was born on Christmas. Christian is the name of my favorite basketball player. Maybe Christian because he's a Christmas baby.

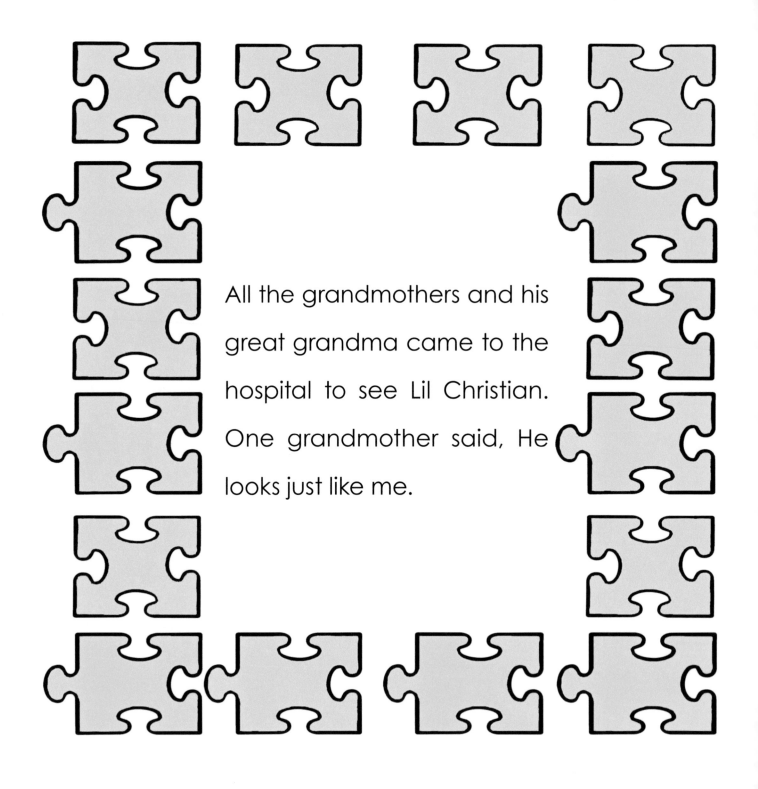

All the grandmothers and his great grandma came to the hospital to see Lil Christian. One grandmother said, He looks just like me.

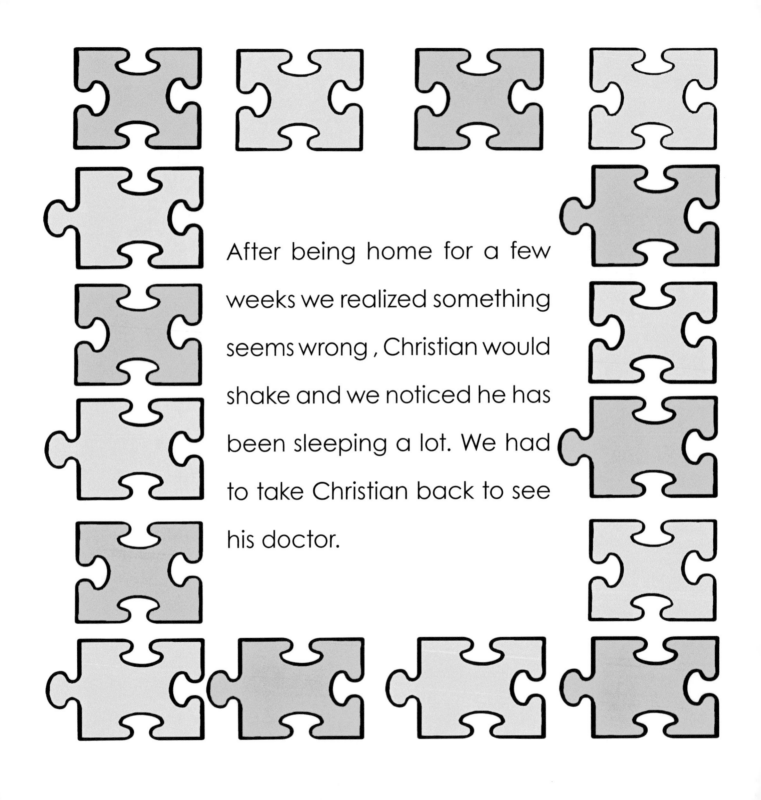

After being home for a few weeks we realized something seems wrong , Christian would shake and we noticed he has been sleeping a lot. We had to take Christian back to see his doctor.

And then we got the news....

Christian is a special child we

were told he has disabilities.

Things went silent.

We were so confused but we have our little joy.

Hang in there Christian, we don't know what's going on but we got you little man said Dad.

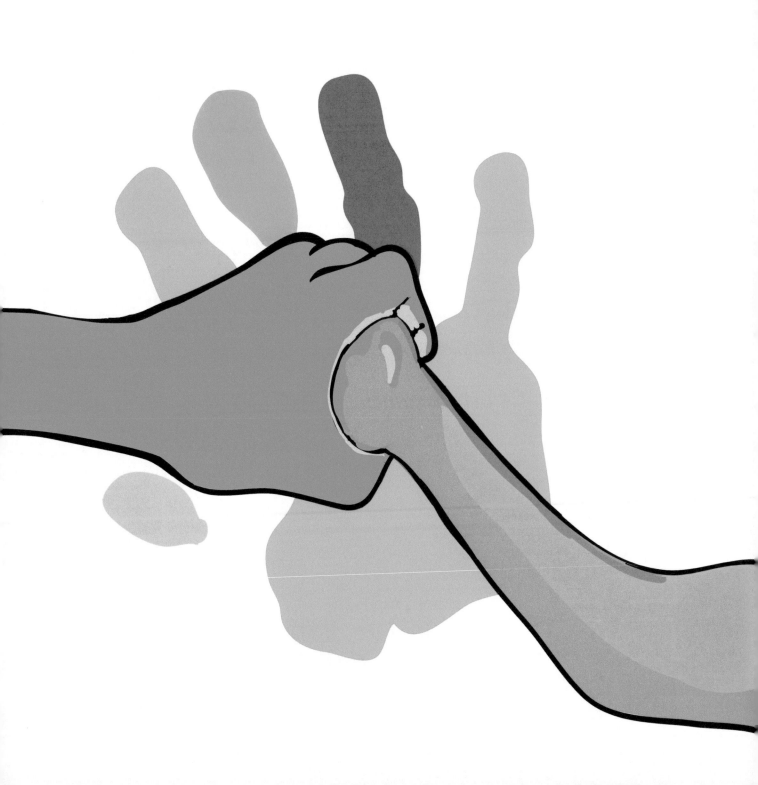

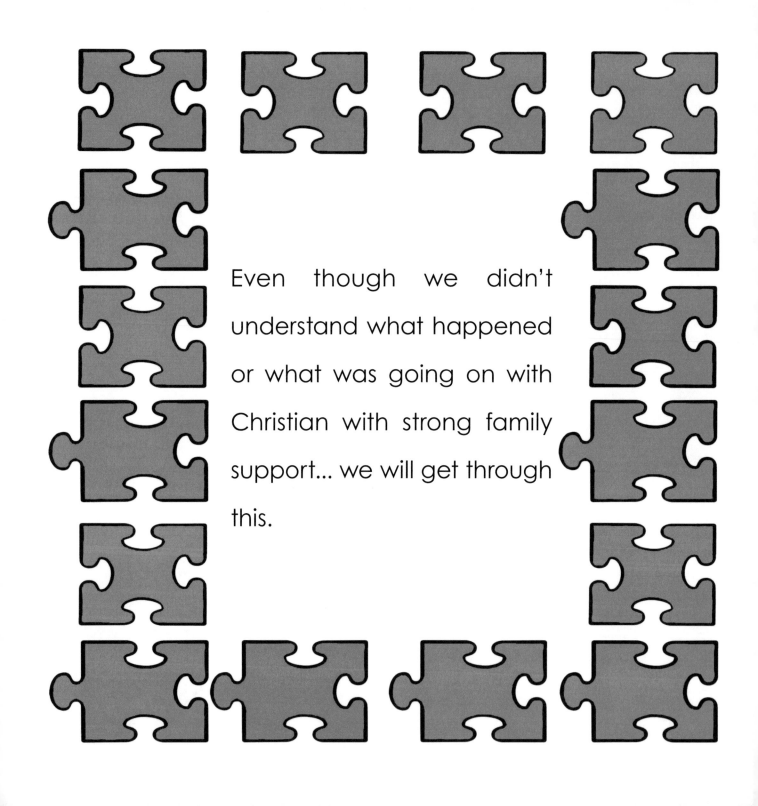

Even though we didn't understand what happened or what was going on with Christian with strong family support... we will get through this.

Christian's little sister Maia was sad and worried but her dad let her know everything will be fine we have to be positive, strong and be supportive for your brother and after that she smiled. Alright then give me high five Daddy.

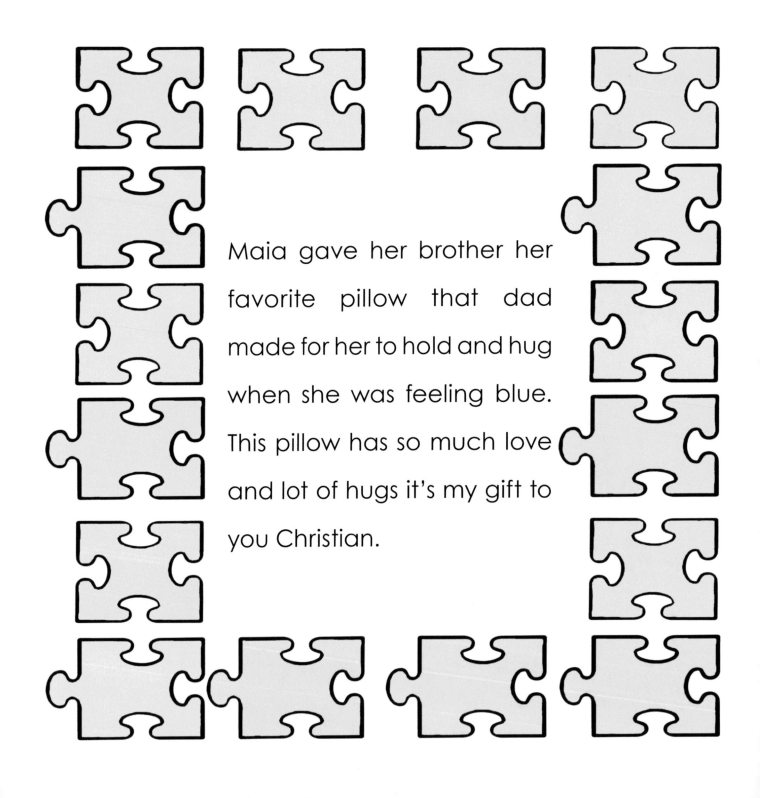

Maia gave her brother her favorite pillow that dad made for her to hold and hug when she was feeling blue. This pillow has so much love and lot of hugs it's my gift to you Christian.

As days, weeks, months and years went by Christian had good days and some not so good. But that never stopped him learning, smiling and going swimming with his friends one of the things he likes to do.

and laughing at his friends

when they were dancing.

With support from family, friends and love ones by your side living with your disabilities can be a good life with a smile.

You will always see me with a cheesy smile and a tight hug with my pillow. You're always welcome for a hug.

Printed in the United States
By Bookmasters